Dear Parent:
Your child's love of readi[illegible].

Every child learns to read in a different way and at his or her own speed. Some go back and forth between reading levels and read favorite books again and again. Others read through each level in order. You can help your young reader improve and become more confident by encouraging his or her own interests and abilities. From books your child reads with you to the first books he or she reads alone, there are I Can Read Books for every stage of reading:

SHARED READING
Basic language, word repetition, and whimsical illustrations, ideal for sharing with your emergent reader

BEGINNING READING
Short sentences, familiar words, and simple concepts for children eager to read on their own

READING WITH HELP
Engaging stories, longer sentences, and language play for developing readers

READING ALONE
Complex plots, challenging vocabulary, and high-interest topics for the independent reader

ADVANCED READING
Short paragraphs, chapters, and exciting themes for the perfect bridge to chapter books

I Can Read Books have introduced children to the joy of reading since 1957. Featuring award-winning authors and illustrators and a fabulous cast of beloved characters, I Can Read Books set the standard for beginning readers.

A lifetime of discovery begins with the magical words **"I Can Read!"**

Visit www.icanread.com for information on enriching your child's reading experience.

For my nieces, Laura and Julia
—H. P.

To Linda and Dave—L. S.

Watercolors and black ink were used to prepare the full-color art.

 Manufactured in China. For information address HarperCollins Children's Books, a division of HarperCollins Publishers, 195 Broadway, New York, NY 10007.
www.icanread.com

Library of Congress Cataloging-in-Publication Data
Parish, Herman.
Amelia Bedelia, cub reporter / by Herman Parish ; pictures by Lynn Sweat.
p. cm.—(I can read! 2 beginning reading)
"Greenwillow Books."
Summary: Amelia Bedelia helps with the school newspaper—to rave reviews.
ISBN 978-0-06-209510-7 (trade ed.)—ISBN 978-0-06-209509-1 (pbk.)
[1. Reporters and reporting—Fiction. 2. Schools—Fiction. 3. Household employees—Fiction.
4. Humorous stories.] I. Sweat, Lynn, ill. II. Title.
PZ7.P2185Aoc 2012 [E]—dc23 2011033655

22 SCP 10 9

Amelia Bedelia, Cub Reporter

story by Herman Parish
pictures by Lynn Sweat

Greenwillow Books
An Imprint of HarperCollins*Publishers*

Amelia Bedelia had just served breakfast.

"Where is the paper?" asked Mr. Rogers.

"Paper?" said Amelia Bedelia.

"What kind of paper would you like?

Notepaper, wallpaper, toilet paper . . ."

"The newspaper," said Mr. Rogers.

"I cannot start my day without it."

"That paper is late," said Amelia Bedelia.

"I'll go and see if it has been delivered."

When Amelia Bedelia opened the front door,

a voice hollered,

Amelia Bedelia did not see any ducks.

The only thing she saw

was a newspaper coming right at her.

Amelia Bedelia ducked

in the nick of time.

BAM! went the paper on the window.

CRASH, clink went the broken glass.

A boy rode his bike up the front walk.

"I am so sorry," he said.

"I am Peter, your paper boy."

“A paper boy?” said Amelia Bedelia.

“You look mighty solid to me.”

“What’s the commotion?” asked Mr. Rogers.

“Are you all right?” asked Mrs. Rogers.

“I am fine,” said Amelia Bedelia.

“Our paper boy broke the window by mistake.”

“Don’t worry, son,” said Mrs. Rogers.

“We will fix it. It is only a small pane.”

“That’s right,” said Amelia Bedelia.

“A larger window is a big pain to fix.”

“I’ll buy a new window,” said Mr. Rogers.

“Let Mrs. Rogers do that,”

said Amelia Bedelia.

“She loves to go window shopping.”

Peter took a camera out of his bag.

“Thanks for not getting mad,” he said.

“May I take your picture for my paper?

We’re doing stories on our best customers.”

Everyone gathered for the picture.

“Cheese!” said Peter.

Amelia Bedelia didn’t see any cheese.

She figured Peter was joking,

so she smiled like Mr. and Mrs. Rogers.

Peter got back on his bike and said,

"I have to deliver the rest of these papers

on my way to school, but now I am late."

"Let me help you," said Amelia Bedelia.

Mrs. Rogers waved and called out,

"Take the rest of the day off."

They made a good team.

Peter carried the papers.

Amelia Bedelia tossed the papers.

She hit every porch

and missed every window.

Peter got to school right on time.

The principal, Mr. Owens,

was outside to greet the students.

Peter introduced Amelia Bedelia to him.

"She knows newspapers," said Peter.

"She could work on the *School Scoop*."

"Then this is our lucky day," said Mr. Owens.

"Our school paper is due out tomorrow,

but the parent who helps with it is ill."

"Would you work with us?" asked Peter.

"Sounds like fun," said Amelia Bedelia.

"That's the spirit," said Mr. Owens.

"Come and meet your cub reporters."

"Cubs?" said Amelia Bedelia.

"I thought the reporters would be kids."

"They are," said Mr. Owens.

"They're called cub reporters

when they're young and new on the job."

When they arrived at the school paper,

Mr. Owens hollered, “Stop the presses!”

A girl looked up, smiled, and said,

“We don’t use printing presses anymore.

We do everything on the computer.”

"I knew that," said Mr. Owens.

"In an old movie I once saw,

the editor yelled 'Stop the presses!'

whenever he found a mistake.

I've always wanted to say that."

The principal introduced Amelia Bedelia.

"Meet your new editor," he said.

"Please send her your stories and photos.

She will write the headlines

and put everything together in the paper."

“Sounds simple,” said Amelia Bedelia.

“Then we print copies for Peter to deliver.”

“No,” said Peter.

“There is no paper boy.

The *School Scoop* is delivered by computer.”

“Peter is right,” said Mr. Owens.

“Our newspaper is available online.”

“Got it,” said Amelia Bedelia.

“I put things on line every day.”

“Excellent,” said the principal.

“Everyone gets a copy instantly—

even my boss, the superintendent.”

SCHOOL SCOOP

As he was leaving,

Mr. Owens gave them some advice.

“To be a good reporter,” he said,

“keep this in mind:

If a dog bites a man, that is not news.

But if a man bites a dog, that is news!”

No one had a clue what he meant.

They all nodded anyway, to be polite.

There was so much going on in the school!

Amelia Bedelia assigned the last story

just as the bell rang for classes to begin.

As the kids filed into the hallway,

Amelia Bedelia gave them some advice, too.

"You cubs be careful! Do not get bitten.

And do not bite any dogs!"

Amelia Bedelia set right to work.

Just when she got used to the school computer,

the stories began to come in.

She wrote a headline for each story.

The library was quieter than usual.
The squeaky rocking chair
used for story time
had been sent out to be repaired.

LIBRARIAN OFF HER ROCKER

During rehearsal
of the school play,
some scenery fell over
onto the actors.

SCHOOL PLAY A BIG HIT

CLICK
At the chess tournament,
both players
moved their knights
early in the game.

KNIGHTS BATTLE IN GYM

CLICK
While he was being interviewed,
the gardening teacher
tripped over a bucket.

GARDENER KICKS THE BUCKET

Two new bear cubs
were spotted
during the zoo field trip.

CUB REPORTERS REPORT ON CUBS

The school nurse
offered every student
the chance to visit her new office.

EVERY KID WILL GET A SHOT

During a fire safety lesson,
the chief said that
he forgot to use sunscreen
on his recent vacation.

FIRE CHIEF BURNED

The eggs incubating
in the fourth grade classrooms
finally hatched.

FOURTH GRADE FULL OF CUTE CHICKS

Amelia Bedelia took a break

to report on a story herself.

On her way back to the office,

she ran into Mr. Owens.

"I did a story on the cafeteria,"

said Amelia Bedelia.

"Great," said Mr. Owens.

"Did you get a hot scoop?"

"I got two scoops," she said,

"but they were both cold."

“That’s too bad,” said the principal.

“Will you still make the deadline?”

“No problem,” said Amelia Bedelia.

“My story is the last one.”

Amelia Bedelia had taste-tested
a different type of hot dog
in the cafeteria.

She was sure
Mr. Owens would love her story.
After all, it was his idea of news.

WOMAN BITES DOG

She hit Send, and the *School Scoop* was on its way to everyone.

The next morning,

Amelia Bedelia returned to tidy up.

Mr. Owens burst into the room.

“Stop the presses!” he yelled.

“Stop the computers! Stop everything!”

“What happened?” asked Amelia Bedelia.

“Is there a big story we need to cover?”

“You bet there is,” said the principal.

“You can report on me getting fired.

My boss is coming here to talk to me

about that newspaper you put out.”

"What's wrong?" asked Amelia Bedelia.

"I published it before the deadline."

"Look at your headlines," said Mr. Owens.

"They are so sensational."

"Thank you," said Amelia Bedelia.

"Don't thank me," Mr. Owens said.

"*That* kind of sensational is not good.

Now our school sounds like a big city."

Before Amelia Bedelia could apologize,
the superintendent burst into the room.
"Mr. Owens! There you are!" she said.
"My phone has been ringing nonstop.
Parents are calling about your newspaper.
They want to know who is responsible."
"I can explain," said Mr. Owens.
"Explain what?" said the superintendent.
"Everyone loves the latest issue!
Parents, teachers, students . . ."
"They do?" said Mr. Owens.
"I mean . . . of course they do!
I knew that!"

“It’s a hit,” the superintendent said.

“Your school sounds exciting and fun.

And those headlines! They are . . . are . . .”

“Sensational?” suggested Amelia Bedelia.

“Exactly!” said the superintendent.

“I roared when I read ‘Woman Bites Dog!’”

“That’s my favorite, too,” said Mr. Owens.

“Meet Amelia Bedelia.

She wrote that.”

“Glad you like it,”

said Amelia Bedelia.

“I wrote it the way I saw it, that’s all.”

"Keep up the good work,"

said the superintendent to Mr. Owens.

"Maybe one day you'll have my job."

"Really?" said Mr. Owens.

"When that happens," said Amelia Bedelia,

"I've got the perfect headline:

'PRINCIPAL BECOMES

SUPER SUPERINTENDENT.'"

After the superintendent left,

Mr. Owens turned to Amelia Bedelia.

"I cannot thank you enough," he said.

"You're sensational—in a good way."

"I knew that," said Amelia Bedelia.

A week later, Mr. and Mrs. Rogers

had just sat down to breakfast

when the doorbell rang.

"Please see who it is," said Mrs. Rogers.

"And see if my paper is here," said Mr. Rogers.

Amelia Bedelia returned with Peter.

“Special delivery,” said Peter.

He handed Mr. Rogers his paper.

“Thank you,” said Mr. Rogers.

“My windows thank you, too.”

“My pleasure,” said Peter.

“I wanted to show you your story.”

Peter held up the front page and said,

"I got to write the article, too."

"Congratulations," said Amelia Bedelia.

"You are not a cub anymore."

THE NEWS
A BREAKING
STORY

"What a clever idea," said Mrs. Rogers.

"A paper boy who broke into reporting . . ."

"By breaking a window," added Mr. Rogers.

"I love your headline," said Amelia Bedelia.

"I couldn't have done better myself."